KILLERS OF THE SACRED MOON

Laura Shenton

KILLERS OF THE SACRED MOON

Laura Shenton

Iridescent Toad Publishing

Iridescent Toad Publishing.

©Laura Shenton 2025
All rights reserved.

Laura Shenton asserts the moral right to be identified as the author of this work.

No part of this publication may be
reproduced, stored or transmitted in any form or by any means, electronic, mechanical, photocopying, recording, scanning, or otherwise without written permission from the publisher. It is illegal to copy this book, post it to a website, or distribute it by any other means without permission.

This book is entirely a work of fiction. The names, characters and incidents portrayed in it are the work of the author's imagination. Any resemblance to actual persons, living or dead, events or localities is entirely coincidental.

Designations used by companies to distinguish their products are often claimed as trademarks. All brand names and product names used in this book and on its cover are trade names, service marks, trademarks and registered trademarks of their respective owners. The publishers and the book are not associated with any product or vendor mentioned in this book. None of the companies referenced within the book have endorsed the book.

Cover by Achlys Book Cover Design.

First edition. ISBN 978-1-913779-06-1

Chapter One

The village of Crow's Perch lay smothered beneath a thick shroud of mist, a forgotten pocket of the world where sunlight rarely dared to trespass. Crooked rooftops jutted up like jagged teeth, and gnarled trees pressed close, their branches twisted and skeletal, clutching at the air as though they could snatch the souls of those who passed beneath. Among the houses, all weathered and sagging, some whispered tales of abandonment, their darkened windows staring blankly, as if challenging the brave to look within. Only the caw of the ravens pierced the silence, their calls low and solemn, as though they alone knew the secrets buried in the shadows.

In the heart of this forsaken place, the old meeting hall stood. It was a crumbling relic, crafted from stone blackened by age and the whispers of curses long forgotten. Inside, four figures gathered, their breaths barely disturbing the musty air. Candles lined the rough stone walls, their flickering flames casting an eerie, shifting light that distorted the shadows, making each figure's face seem haunted, as though they were all hiding something.

Voss stood at the head of the room. He was tall, built with the hardened edges of a man who had seen – and caused – death in every conceivable form. Scars marred his rough skin, tracing paths along his jaw and disappearing beneath the collar of his worn leather coat. He observed the others, lingering longest on the elder beside him.

"Speak plainly," Voss declared. "We know why we're here."

The elder – a skeletal, gaunt man who seemed more a shade than flesh – stepped forward. His skin was ashen, and his eyes were lost in hollows that gave him a haunted look.

"The sacred moon has risen again," he

announced, his voice as thin as spider silk. "We had hoped it would not. Yet here we are, bound by ancient duty."

Orin shifted uneasily. He was younger than Voss, with a mane of dark, unruly hair and a smirk that hid behind an ever-present layer of scepticism. Despite his role as the group's mage, he was no wizard from fables of old. His magic was raw, barely tamed, and dark like the nights he had spent wandering through his own regrets.

"Ancient duty," he scoffed softly. "What does that mean in a place like this? Just tell us what we're supposed to kill."

Beside him, Lira was silent, her eyes cast downward as though in prayer. Her face was obscured by a hood, but her gaze, when it rose, held the sharpness of a blade. Ravens seemed drawn to her; one perched on the windowsill behind her, staring with an unnerving intelligence.

The elder's lips twisted into a half-smile, humourless and full of sorrow.

"The moon is sacred, but also cursed," he

murmured. "Bound to a creature – a beast older than the stones of this village. It rises with the moon, hunting. It claims the lives of those who dare to walk beneath its watch, and it is growing restless."

Voss exhaled slowly, his hand curling around the hilt of the sword at his side. He had expected trouble, but nothing could have prepared him for the palpable weight in the air, the sheer intensity of something ancient and bleak that seemed to press down on him.

"So, we kill the beast and break the curse," he said matter-of-factly.

"It isn't that simple," the elder countered. "It never is. Many have tried. None have returned."

The elder lowered his gaze, as if retreating into some distant memory. A chill settled over the group. Orin looked away, the smirk vanishing from his face to be replaced by a grim line. Lira remained silent, her hand resting lightly on the bow slung across her shoulder, her fingers grazing the quiver of arrows as though reassured by their presence.

"It claims souls," the elder continued, his voice barely a whisper. "The moon drinks them. This creature is its guardian and its prisoner."

"Then it is no mere beast," Orin muttered suspiciously. "It's something worse."

"We'll do what we must," said Lira, her voice soft yet edged with something unyielding. "Or it will be the village that pays the price."

She glanced at the raven on the windowsill, and it tilted its head as though in acknowledgment, its black eyes glinting.

The elder nodded, his bony hand reaching into his robes and pulling forth a crumpled map stained with age. He unfolded it, his hands shaking slightly, as though even the memory of the forest that lay beyond the village unnerved him. The map showed winding paths, marked with symbols of warning, skulls drawn in the margins, as if the paper itself held the cries of those lost in the woods. At the centre was a single mark – a black circle drawn where the trees grew thickest.

"This is where you'll find it," the elder said, pointing a trembling finger at the heart of the forest. "The clearing of the sacred moon."

"When?" Voss demanded, taking hold of the map to study it.

"Tonight," the elder urged, his voice nearly breaking. "When the moon is at its peak."

With a decisive grunt, Voss turned to address Lira and Orin.

"We leave at once," he commanded. "The longer we wait, the worse it could get. Prepare yourselves."

Orin grumbled something to himself, but obeyed, checking the vials of potion strapped to his belt and testing the edge of his dagger. Lira stood still, fixed on the raven, which continued to watch her with judgment. She murmured something under her breath, barely audible, and the raven gave a soft croak in response before taking flight into the mist.

The trio left the hall, stepping into the streets. Fog clung to them as they walked, curling around their legs as though reluctant to let them pass. The villagers peered out from behind doorways and shutters, eyes fearful, knowing what this night would most likely bring, aware that most who walked the path beneath the sacred moon did not return.

As the group passed the final house, a child's voice broke the silence.

"Will you come back?"

Voss stopped, turning to see a small girl standing by the edge of the road, her eyes wide and unblinking. He looked down at her, making a conscious decision to be stoic and reassuring in his response. He then nodded once, a slow and solemn promise that was more precarious than he cared to acknowledge.

"Yes," he murmured. "We'll come back."

But as the mist swallowed them and ravens circled overhead, cawing a warning that echoed through the stillness, Voss felt the uncertainty settle within his gut. He knew, on this night, with the sacred moon rising, promises were as fragile as glass.

Chapter Two

The forest loomed ahead, a dense wall of trees that twisted and contorted as if frozen in the middle of a monstrous dance. The mist clung to the ground in thick patches, rising in ghostly tendrils as Voss and his companions entered, their every step muffled and swallowed by the loamy earth beneath. Shadows flitted between the trunks, shapeless and fleeting, giving the group the unsettling impression that they were being watched by hundreds of unseen eyes.

Orin was the first to break the silence, his voice barely more than a mutter:

"This place feels like it's breathing."

Lira walked a few paces ahead, her bow at the ready, fingers brushing the fletching of an arrow. She didn't respond, but remained alert, every flicker in the mist and rustle of leaves drawing her attention. Voss could see the tension in her posture, the coiled readiness of a hunter anticipating the strike of her prey – or perhaps her own death.

The group moved in a loose formation, each person watching a different angle, their senses stretched taut as wire. Above them, ravens croaked from the high branches, their dark forms like shards of midnight scattered among the leaves. Voss glanced up as one swooped low, passing close enough that he could feel the whisper of its wings, a macabre omen in the shape of a bird.

"Ravens," Orin murmured, his gaze following the birds. "Aren't they supposed to be messengers of the dead?"

"Messengers and guides," Lira replied, her voice quiet but sharp. "They watch us. They wait."

"If we're lucky, they'll only be watching," said Voss, looking ahead, his focus unwavering.

But as they pressed deeper into the forest, luck felt like a fragile hope. The trees grew denser and the air took on an abundant, cloying weight, thick with the scent of damp earth and something else – something metallic, almost like blood. The forest was darker here, as though even the moonlight refused to pierce through the rich canopy.

Finally, they reached a break in the trees, a small clearing surrounded by twisted trunks and roots that seemed to reach out, clawing at the air. In the centre of the clearing lay an old stone altar, weathered and covered in a thin film of moss. Ancient runes, faint but still visible, were carved into its surface, forming a strange language that curled and writhed in ways no human hand could have written.

Orin approached it first, suspicion on his face as he examined the runes.

"I've seen markings like these before, but never this ancient," he said as he traced a finger along the grooves, his brow furrowing. "It could be a binding spell, or a summoning, perhaps, but the language is older than any I've studied."

"The elder said the creature was bound to the

sacred moon," Voss said with caution. "Could this be where it was... summoned?"

"Bound, summoned – it's difficult to tell with spells like these," said Orin. "But this isn't some wild beast. This is something crafted, something given purpose and tethered to it. Someone put it here, and I doubt they did it out of kindness."

"Who would bind a creature like that?" Lira asked, her gaze fixed on the altar.

Orin shrugged, his fingers brushing over the runes as if to test their strength.

"Someone with more power than sense, most likely," he said. "Magic like this – it comes at a cost. You don't imprison something powerful without leaving a piece of yourself behind."

A cold silence fell over the group. The altar seemed to throb as though its ancient energy refused to relent, refused to fade. Lira took a step back, her fingers tightening around her bow, and Voss felt a prickling sensation running along his skin, the undeniable feeling of being watched.

Chapter Two

They had barely turned to leave when a guttural growl came from the trees. It was a sound that vibrated through the earth, clipped yet hollow, like the voice of the forest itself coming alive to meet them. The shadows seemed to gather, pulling together into something solid, something with form.

Voss' grip tightened on his sword, every muscle in his body tensing.

"Form up," he ordered.

The group fell into a defensive stance, backs to one another as they faced the shifting shadows. Orin raised his hand, a subtle luminescence forming at his fingertips as he murmured an incantation under his breath. Lira knocked an arrow, her gaze fixed on the black miasma that swirled around them.

The growl came again, closer this time, resonating in their bones. Within the haze, a pair of gleaming eyes appeared, crimson and unblinking, but the creature's form remained indistinct, a mass of darkness that seemed to shift and writhe. Its intent, however, was clear: a predator watching its prey.

The creature's gaze fixed on Voss, and an icy chill ran through him, sharp and unrelenting. He felt as though he was being seen in a way no mortal eyes could perceive. The creature wasn't merely watching him: it was probing, its presence reaching deep into him, peeling back the layers of his soul as though searching for something to latch onto.

"Voss," Orin whispered urgently, "don't look at it. It'll try to get inside your head."

Voss tore his gaze away, breaking the creature's hold, but the sense of violation lingered. He forced himself to focus, feeling the weight of his sword in his hand, grounding himself in the here and now.

"What is this thing?" he asked.

"Bound by blood, freed by fate," Orin muttered, a tremor in his voice. "That's what the elder said. That thing... it's a guardian. But it's not here to protect us."

"Then let's send it back to whatever forsaken place it came from," said Lira, taking aim and drawing her bowstring taut.

She released the arrow, and it sliced through the air, its fletching gleaming in the moonlight as it shot towards the creature. There was a sickening thud as it struck, the point sinking into the darkness. For a moment, the creature's form wavered, and a horrific sound – a strangled, guttural scream – filled the air, causing the ravens above to caw in fright.

Instead of retreating, however, the creature's form grew more defined, its shape solidifying as though strangely nurtured by the attack. Shadows gathered around it, condensing into twisted limbs and a face that stretched into an unnatural smile, teeth glinting in a grotesque mockery of a human grin.

Orin recoiled in horror.

"It feeds off magic, off violence," he said. "We're giving it strength."

"Then how do we kill it?" Voss pressed.

The creature lunged with inhuman speed. Voss barely had time to raise his sword before it was upon him, its claws scraping against the steel with a sound like nails on stone. Instinctively, he parried.

Lira fired again, aiming for the creature's head, but it contorted, the arrow passing through its form as though it was made of mist. Orin began chanting, his voice a steady rhythm, building power with each word as the light at his fingertips brightened, illuminating the darkness around them.

The creature's gaze locked onto him, and it darted his way, moving with a grace and speed belying its mysterious form. Before the creature could strike, a burst of light erupted from Orin's hand. It seared the creature with a flash of silver, making it recoil and hiss, its form unravelling slightly as tendrils of blackness faded away like smoke.

"Whatever this thing is," Orin said breathily, "it doesn't like silver."

Voss gritted his teeth, feeling his resolve settle over him.

"Then we'll give it more silver than it can handle."

As the creature began to reform, they braced themselves, weapons at the ready, knowing that the fight had only just begun.

Chapter Three

The forest grew darker as they pressed on, each step tense after their encounter with the creature. Mist curled around their ankles, thick as smoke, and above them, the branches tangled like twisted fingers, barely letting in slivers of the sacred moon's light. Every so often, the mournful cry of a raven pierced the air, as though the birds were invested in the fate of the forest, waiting for the next move.

Voss led the way, his jaw set, his hand resting on the hilt of his sword. Though he kept his face blank, every fibre of his being was on edge. The experience with the creature had left its mark on him, a lingering sense of violation that clung to his skin like oil. He could feel something watching, even now, slipping through the trees like a ghostly fog, unseen but present.

Lira was close behind, alert and unblinking, like a predator tracking its prey. She hadn't spoken since they'd left the clearing, but Voss could feel her intensity, the sharp focus that radiated from her like a cold flame.

Orin, limping slightly, glanced around nervously, his fingers twitching at his side. His confidence seemed to have drained away, replaced by a wary suspicion that clung to him like the mist. He muttered softly to himself, an incantation or a prayer perhaps.

At last, they paused to catch their breath, gathering in a small glade where the moonlight broke through in pale beams, casting eerie silhouettes that danced on the ground. Voss took a moment to study his companions.

"We're not dealing with a simple creature here," he said finally. "Whatever this thing is, it's got intelligence. It's watching us, waiting for us to slip."

"I agree," said Orin, clenching his fists. "It's an ancient magic, something far older than anything I've encountered before. I can feel it in the air – it's as if the entire forest is alive, feeding off our fear. But it's vulnerable to

Chapter Three

silver, that much we know. There's always a way to break a curse."

"Silver might hurt it," Lira murmured, "but to kill it? We'll need more than that."

As they prepared to move on, a familiar sound caught their attention: the cawing of ravens, louder this time, more insistent. Voss looked up, scanning the treetops, and froze as he saw them: a line of ravens perched along the branches, their eyes glinting like black jewels in the moonlight. They were watching him, silent and still, as though bearing witness to something vital.

Orin shivered, looking up and nodding in the direction of the ravens.

"Are they... following us?" he uttered.

"Kind of," Lira confirmed, giving a slight nod. "They're not here for us though. They're here for what's coming."

The words hung in the air, chilling in their simplicity. Voss swallowed, his throat dry, and forced himself to turn away from the ravens, focusing on the path ahead. They had come too far to turn back now, and whatever lay ahead was bound to reveal itself soon enough.

They continued in silence, the forest growing thicker around them, pressing in like a living entity. The air was heavy with the scent of damp earth and decay, a cloying sweetness that filled their lungs and made each breath feel like a struggle. Shadows danced at the edges of their vision, flickering in and out of existence, teasing them with glimpses of movement.

The ground beneath their feet grew increasingly uneven, roots twisting and curling like the knuckles of some ancient, buried beast. Voss stumbled, catching himself against a tree, his hand pressing against the rough bark. As he pulled away, he noticed something strange: symbols carved into the wood, subtle but unmistakable, glowing faintly in the dim light.

Orin moved closer, tracing the symbols with a fingertip.

"These... these are wards," he said, awe and trepidation mingling in his voice. "Old magic, to keep something contained."

"Contained where?" Voss asked cautiously, frowning and glancing around. "We're deep in the forest. There's nothing here but trees and mist."

"These wards... they're not meant to protect us," Orin explained, shaking his head, his expression grave. "They're meant to prevent something from getting out."

A chill ran down Voss' spine. He could feel it again, that presence lurking just beyond sight, slipping through the gloom like a living nightmare. The air grew colder, a biting sharpness that seeped into his bones, and he gripped the hilt of his sword tighter, grounding himself in the solidity of the steel.

"It's watching us," said Lira.

Before Voss could respond, a rustling came from the trees, and a shape emerged. It was the creature, more defined now, its form solidifying in the moonlight. Its eyes gleamed, dark and unblinking, and a grotesque grin stretched across its face, a mockery of human expression.

The creature took a step forward, its movements slow and deliberate, as though savouring the terror that rippled through the group. Voss felt his pulse quicken, but he forced himself to stand his ground, meeting the creature's gaze with steely determination.

"You're not going to scare us off," he said with a growl, his voice steady despite the fear gnawing at him.

The creature's grin widened, its eyes flicking between them with an unsettling intelligence. It raised a clawed hand, pointing at Voss, and a voice – soft but powerful – echoed in his mind.

"Bound by blood, freed by fate."

The words hit Voss like a blow, the intensity of them pressing into his mind, filling his thoughts with images of blood and bleak endings. He could feel something pulling at him, a force that seemed to reach into his very soul, as though seeking to bind him to something dreadful.

Orin's voice broke through the haze, sharp and urgent:

"Voss! Snap out of it!"

Chapter Three

Voss blinked, shaking his head to clear his mind. The creature's gaze lingered on him for a moment longer before it turned its attention to Orin, its grin widening. Shadows coiled around it, twisting and writhing as it began to shift, its form blurring and stretching.

"We end this now," Lira declared, raising her bow.

She loosed an arrow, the silver tip gleaming as it cut through the air. The creature shrieked as it struck, its form shuddering, fragments of darkness peeling away like smoke. But the creature did not retreat; it only seemed to grow stronger, its shape becoming more defined, more human.

Orin drew a small vial from his belt, the liquid inside a luminous, vibrant blue.

"This should hold it back, at least for a moment."

He flung the vial at the creature. It shattered on impact, the liquid splattering with a sharp hiss. The creature recoiled instantly, its form scattering in a fleeting burst.

"Run!" Orin shouted, his voice tight with urgency. "It won't hold for long!"

They turned and fled, their feet pounding against the earth as they raced deeper into the forest. The creature's shrieks followed them, echoing through the trees, a haunting reminder that they were now being hunted. Voss could feel the creature's anger, a palpable force that clung to them, pressing down like the hand of some malevolent god.

As they ran, the ravens took flight, their cries filling the air, merging with the creature's wails into a frantic cacophony. Shadows twisted and writhed around them, reaching out with an almost violent aura, and Voss could feel the forest itself closing in, a living, breathing entity that wanted nothing more than to consume them.

But they pushed on, their breaths coming in ragged gasps, their footsteps unsteady as they stumbled through the darkness. Voss could feel his strength waning, the ache in his body increasing mercilessly, but he forced himself to keep going, driven by a single, unyielding thought: they had to survive.

Chapter Four

Voss' heart pounded as he pushed forward, his senses straining to catch any sound of pursuit. Behind him, Orin and Lira kept pace, each driven by the raw, primal instinct for self-preservation. It was more than fear that urged them onward; it was the knowledge that something far older and darker was bearing down on them, a force bound to the sacred moon, relentless and unforgiving.

A raven's call echoed above, sharp and commanding. Voss looked up to see the large bird flying ahead, its wings slicing through the mist with ease. It seemed to guide them, weaving through the trees with a grace that bordered on supernatural. Lira noticed it too, her gaze sharpening as she tracked the bird's path, as though taking cues from its movements.

"Follow it," she urged. "It's trying to lead us somewhere."

"And we trust a bird now?" Orin countered, casting a doubtful glance upward. "In case you missed it, those things have been watching us since we set foot in this forest."

"It's leading us away from the creature," Lira insisted, her tone leaving no room for argument. "And right now, that's enough."

Reluctantly, Orin nodded, and they fell into line behind Lira, following the raven as it swooped through the trees. From behind them, they could hear the creature's guttural shrieks, distorted and distant, but growing closer with each passing moment. Voss could feel its presence closing in, oppressive and unrelenting.

They stumbled into another clearing, the moonlight pooling on the ground like liquid silver. The raven perched on a low branch, watching them with its beady, intelligent eyes, as though appraising their every move. Voss took a moment to catch his breath, scanning the area for any sign of the creature.

"What now?" Orin said, panting and looking around warily. "We can't keep running like this. We need a plan."

"Yes," Voss agreed, his mind racing. "If it's vulnerable to silver, we can use that to our advantage. Orin, do you have any more of that potion?"

Orin shook his head, a grimace contorting his features.

"That was my last vial. But this might buy us some time, if we get close enough."

He reached into his pack, pulling out a silver dagger, its blade dull but still glinting in the moonlight.

Lira examined the weapon thoughtfully.

"It's better than nothing," she said. "If we can draw the creature into the open, we might have a chance. But we'll need bait."

A heavy silence fell over the group as Lira's words sank in. She looked pointedly at Voss, an unpleasant understanding passing between them. He knew what she was suggesting, and he knew there was no other choice.

"I'll do it," he said, his voice steady. "You two stay here, and when it comes for me, you strike."

Orin opened his mouth to protest, but the look in Voss' eyes deterred him. Voss had made up his mind, and there was no room for debate. He handed Orin the map, his fingers lingering for a moment, a reminder of the path they would need to take if he didn't make it back.

"Don't waste time," Voss murmured. "If it goes wrong, you run. Don't look back."

Lira's expression softened for a fleeting moment, a glimmer of deep respect in her eyes.

"We won't let it take you," she promised firmly.

Voss nodded, and then turned away, forcing himself to ignore the tightness in his chest, the dread that threatened to consume him. He stepped out into the clearing, the cold light of the sacred moon washing over him, casting long, ominous patterns that stretched across the ground.

Chapter Four

The creature's howl broke through the silence, closer now. Voss braced himself, every nerve on edge as the darkness around him thickened, coalescing into a shape that slithered out from the trees, its red eyes fixed on him with a hunger beyond mortal comprehension.

The creature moved with unnatural grace, its hazy form shifting and writhing, mingling with the air. Voss held his ground, his hand resting on the hilt of his sword, his gaze locked onto the creature's eyes. He could feel it probing at his mind again, its presence worming into his thoughts, searching for weakness.

"Is this all you've got?" he muttered, a flicker of defiance sparking within him. "I've faced worse nightmares than you."

The creature paused, its crooked grin widening, as though amused by its opponent's bravado. Shadows curled around it, charcoal tendrils stretching out like skeletal fingers. Voss could feel the cold grip of fear, but he held his position, refusing to give the creature the satisfaction of seeing him flinch.

Behind him, he could hear the faint rustling of leaves as Orin and Lira positioned themselves, ready and waiting to strike. He knew they didn't want to fail him, and that they were skilled, determined. But he also knew that facing a creature like this required more than ability and courage. It required sacrifice, the willingness to give something of oneself.

The creature lunged, its claws slicing through the air, and Voss dodged to the side, his movements quick and precise. He swung his sword, the blade catching the moonlight as it sliced through the night, but the creature twisted, evading the strike with inhuman agility. It circled him, its eyes gleaming with cruel intelligence, as though savouring the hunt.

Voss knew he couldn't keep this up for long. His strength was waning, his muscles burning with the effort of each movement. He needed to draw it closer, to give Orin and Lira the opening they needed. He took a step back, reminding himself to be calm and focused despite the dire circumstances.

And then, he saw it: the faint glint of silver

Chapter Four

from behind the creature, the slight movement that signalled Orin's approach. Voss locked eyes with the creature, his lips curling into a wry smile.

"Come on, then," he taunted, his voice a low growl. "Let's finish this."

The creature lunged again, and this time, Voss didn't move. He remained rooted to the spot, grimacing as the creature's claws raked across his chest, the impact knocking the breath from his lungs. Pain exploded through him, sharp and searing, but he forced himself to stay upright, to stay fixed on the creature's eyes, to hold its attention.

In that split second, Orin struck. The silver dagger plunged into the creature's back, and a scream, sharp and piercing, tore through the air, reverberating through the trees. The creature's form convulsed, its body shuddering as the silver burned through it, tendrils of darkness peeling away like smoke.

Lira loosed an arrow, its silver tip striking the creature's head with deadly precision. Another scream rang out through the forest, louder this time, as the creature's form continued to unravel, its twisted shape finally collapsing in on itself and dissipating into nothingness.

Voss staggered back, clutching his chest, his breathing ragged. He could feel the blood soaking through his shirt, crimson and warm, but he forced himself to stay on his feet, his gaze fixed on the spot where the creature had been.

"Did we kill it?" Orin asked shakily, moving to stand by Voss' side.

"It looks that way," Voss replied, shaking his head, "but I'm not convinced. I've got a horrible feeling in my gut that this isn't over."

Lira approached, her expression grim as she surveyed the clearing.

"We need to break the curse in its entirety," she said. "Permanently."

The enormity of the task before them was undeniable. There was no turning back now. From what they had seen, the only choice was to face the curse, to sever the bond that tied the creature to the moon.

Chapter Four

As they turned to leave the clearing, a raven on a high branch let out a final, haunting cry, its voice carrying through the stillness like a warning. Voss looked up, watching as it spread its wings and took flight, its shape vanishing into the mist.

***

Burdened by their injuries and the knowledge that their struggle was far from over, the group's path back to the village was slower. Voss kept his hand pressed against his chest, feeling the steady rhythm of his heartbeat beneath his fingers, a reminder that he was still alive, that he still had the strength left to face what awaited them.

Orin walked beside him, seeming distant, as though lost in thought. The events of the brutal night had stripped away his bravado, leaving behind only the raw, unguarded expression of a man who had glimpsed something beyond his understanding. Voss could sense his terror, the doubt that gnawed at him, but he said nothing, knowing that each of them carried their own hardships.

Lira moved ahead, her steps steady despite the blood that streaked her arm where something had grazed her. Her face was set in sombre determination, focused on the road before her, as though she could already see the next battle that lay in wait. Voss watched her, a strange sense of admiration stirring within him. She had not wavered once, even in the face of the creature's terror, and he knew that her strength would be crucial in the fight to come.

As they neared the edge of the forest, the first faint hint of dawn touched the sky, casting a pale light over the trees. The mist began to lift, swirling away like a veil, and Voss felt a strange sense of release, as though the forest itself was letting them go, relinquishing its hold on them for the brief respite of day.

But even as they emerged into the open, he could feel the sacred moon lingering over them, a reminder that the curse was far from broken, that the creature was only one piece of a more sinister puzzle.

They paused, each of them casting one last look back at the forest, at the twisted shapes of the trees that loomed like sentinels, watching them leave. Voss took a deep breath and then turned to face his companions.

Chapter Four

"We mustn't allow ourselves to be fooled by the presence of daylight," he said, his voice quiet but resolute. "As long as it's bound to the moon, the curse is ever present."

"Indeed," said Orin. "If we want to end this, we need to sever the bond. And that means returning to the heart of the curse."

"There's no avoiding it," Lira said stoically. "We'll have to face the forest again, and soon."

Chapter Five

By the time the group returned to Crow's Perch, the village was stirring awake, though its inhabitants moved with the wary caution of people who had lived too long under the cloak of fear. Villagers peeked out from behind weather-beaten shutters and doorways, their faces gaunt, their mannerisms resigned. It was clear that few held hope for the hunters' success; those who dared venture outside kept their heads down, eyes averted, as though any glimpse of the returning group might invite the curse upon them.

Voss, Lira and Orin made their way to the meeting hall, each step a reminder of the toll their battle had taken. Orin was nursing bruises and cuts, his expression drained and haunted, while Lira moved stiffly, her arm wrapped in a crude bandage made from the hem of her cloak. Voss' wounds throbbed, but he ignored the pain, his mind focused on the next steps.

Inside the hall, the village elder awaited them, his frail form draped in rich, obsidian robes. His attention lingered on each of them, taking in their injuries, the blood that marked their clothes, and the hardened expressions etched into their faces. There was a flicker of something in his gaze – a blend of respect and worry – as he inclined his head in greeting.

"You've returned," he said, his voice sombre. "I had thought... I had feared..."

"We wounded the creature," Voss interrupted, his tone edged with frustration. "But it's not dead. Whatever curse binds it to the sacred moon, it's still intact. If we're to finish this, we need to know the details."

The elder appeared wary, his fingers kneading the fabric of his robes. He looked away, as though ashamed.

"The truth is a dangerous thing," he finally said. "Some curses are born of choices we cannot undo."

Chapter Five

"Then it's time you told us about those choices," Orin insisted, scoffing bitterly. "You owe us that much."

The elder's face tightened, his shoulders slumping under Orin's words.

"You're right," he said apologetically, resignation in his tone. "This isn't just some mindless beast: it's bound, by blood and fate. Indeed, that creature was once human. Long ago, he was one of our own – a guardian who swore to protect this village, to keep the darkness at bay. But in his zeal, he sought power beyond human understanding, power that twisted him into something monstrous."

"And the village let that happen?" Lira demanded angrily. "You knew what he had become, and you bound him here, to the moon?"

"Indeed," said the elder, a flicker of shame crossing his face. "The elders before my time believed that by binding him to the sacred moon, they could contain the curse, use his power to shield the village from other threats. It worked – for a time. But the cost was far greater than they could have foreseen. The moon drank his soul, twisted it into something that lives on even now."

Voss frowned, realising that their mission was far more complex – and dangerous – than he had anticipated. This was to be no simple hunt, but an exorcism – a breaking of bonds that had been forged through blood and ancient rites.

"If we're to end this," Voss said slowly, choosing his words carefully, "we need a way to sever that bond. How was the ritual performed?"

"The rite was lost to us long ago," the elder replied hesitantly. "But there is a way, a dangerous path that no one has dared to attempt. To sever the bond, one must confront the spirit directly – weaken it enough to break its hold over the moon."

"Confront it?" Orin voiced incredulously, unable to conceal his frustration. "And how exactly are we meant to do that without being torn apart?"

"If you truly wish to break the curse, you must return to the clearing tonight, under the sacred moon's full light," said the elder, his expression hardening. "Only in the presence of the moon can the spirit be summoned fully. And you must bring something of great sacrifice – something that holds meaning to the spirit, something it values."

Voss clenched his jaw, a deep unease settling over him. He had seen many cursed places in his time, but this was different. This curse was woven into the very essence of the village, a sinister veil that clung to every stone, every fragment.

"And if we fail?" he asked, his voice quiet with caution.

"Then the curse will only grow stronger," the elder said regretfully. "It will continue to claim the lives of those who wander under the sacred moon."

Voss shuddered at the enormity of the elder's words, at the knowledge that failure would mean death – not just for him and his companions, but eventually for every soul in Crow's Perch. He looked to Lira and Orin, seeing their resolve, the same furious determination that burned within him.

"We have no choice, then," he said eventually. "Tonight, we end this."

The elder bowed his head, a solemn expression etched into his lined face.

"May the gods guide you," he murmured. "And may the moon show mercy."

As they turned to leave, Lira paused, casting a long, searching look at the elder.

"One last question," she said, sharp as steel. "Why have you never tried to break the curse yourselves?"

For a moment, a flicker of something crossed the elder's face – something that looked suspiciously like guilt.

"Because the curse demands blood," he said uncomfortably. "And none of us were willing to pay that price."

With that, he turned away, retreating into the gloom, leaving the trio alone.

They stepped out into the pale daylight, the air carrying the scent of damp earth and decay. The village lay silent, its buildings casting long silhouettes across the cobblestones, as if pointing towards the path ahead.

"So that's it, then?" said Orin. "We're offering ourselves up as sacrifices, for those too afraid to take responsibility for the curse?"

"Not necessarily," Lira said, thoughtful and calm. "We do this for ourselves, not for them. For the chance to end the cycle, to stop the curse from claiming more lives. That's all the reason we need."

Voss nodded, his mind set. He knew the path ahead would be fraught with danger, that the creature they had faced in the night was no mere monster, but the embodiment of a curse born of human greed and betrayal. He also knew there was no other option; the sacred moon awaited them, a silent witness to the battle that would decide the fate of them all.

"We've done all we can for now," he said. "The forest won't wait for us to be ready, and we'll need every ounce of strength for what's coming. We rest now – properly – or we'll regret it when the sun sets. Get some sleep."

***

Later that day, as the sun began its slow descent, casting the village in a subtle, fading glow, the group made their final preparations. They sharpened their weapons, checked their supplies, and steeled themselves for the night to come. Over a simple but hearty meal at the tavern where they had slept, they ate in silence, each bite an acknowledgement of the strength they would need, their unspoken fears tainting their every movement. As darkness fell, a raven perched on one of the wooden beams, its eyes gleaming with a knowing look, as though it understood the path they would soon walk.

When the moon finally rose, casting its unforgiving light over Crow's Perch, the trio set off into the forest once more, their shadows stretching behind them.

Chapter Six

The forest was different under the full light of the sacred moon. It breathed, a subtle, shifting presence that seemed to reach out to Voss, Lira and Orin as they ventured deeper. Moonbeams filtered down in pale, sickly streaks, casting a silver sheen that twisted the branches into clawed hands and painted the mist in ghostly shades. Every tree held the essence of centuries, the air thick with the scent of dampness and rot.

The group walked in silence, each step measured, their senses stretched to almost breaking point. The forest felt alive, pressing in around them, a malevolent force that thrummed with the dark energy of the sacred moon. Ravens flitted between branches, their knowing, obsidian eyes reflecting the light, watching with an unnerving stillness. Lira's gaze followed them, her expression difficult to decipher, though Voss could see the tension in her shoulders, the guarded conversation she seemed to share with the birds.

At last, Orin broke the silence, his voice a strained whisper:

"Do you feel it? The air: it's... thick, like it's trying to suffocate us."

"Yes," said Voss, keeping his attention straight ahead. "Evidently, the curse binds this place."

He paused to check the map the elder had given them, tracing their route with a calloused finger.

"We're close now," he said. "The clearing should be just beyond those trees."

"Whatever we face tonight, it won't let us go easily," Lira murmured, tightening her fingers around her bow. "The curse demands blood, and it will claim it."

They pushed forward until even the sound of their own breathing seemed to be swallowed by obscurity. The light grew brighter, more intense, as though the sacred moon was watching, frigid and foreboding as the forest opened up ahead of them to reveal the clearing.

In the centre of the clearing stood the ancient stone altar, the runes carved into its surface illuminated by a faint, eerie light. The stones around it, cracked and weathered, seemed to throb with energy, their jagged edges gleaming like teeth. Mist curled around the altar, almost opaque, its presence distorting everything and making the shadows twist and dance.

Voss approached the altar slowly, feeling the presence of the curse settling over him like a physical entity, pressing down on his shoulders and making each step a struggle. He reached out, brushing his fingers against the rough surface of the stone, feeling a strange, pulsing warmth beneath. The runes flared, casting brief flashes of light that seemed to seep into his skin, leaving behind a tingling, almost electric sensation.

Orin moved beside him, his expression one of awe and trepidation.

"These runes... they're alive," he murmured, tracing the ancient symbols with his hand. "Bound by magic that is neither living nor dead, tied to the moon's cycle. This is no ordinary curse – it's a bond, one that reaches into the very heart of the sacred moon."

"Then how do we break it?" Voss demanded, frowning, his hand still hovering over the stone.

"Breaking it would mean severing the bond to the moon itself," said Orin. "It's a power beyond any spell I know. The only way would be to sever the soul tied to the curse. The creature itself is the bond."

Lira's focus remained fixed on the bleakness that lingered at the edge of the clearing, her posture rigid.

"Then we draw it out," she uttered, steady, calm. "We make it come to us, and we face it, here, under the light of the moon."

The forest seemed to hold its breath in anticipation. Voss could feel it building, an unpleasant energy that pulsed through the air, abundant and charged. He knew that this night would end only one way – with blood, and with the curse either broken or claimed anew.

"Let's set up," he said. "Orin, mark the ground around the altar. Having a boundary in place could prove crucial."

Orin nodded, pulling a small pouch of salt and herbs from his bag. He sprinkled a line around the altar, chanting softly under his breath, the words a blend of old spells and protective charms, woven together to form a circle of binding. The salt glowed faintly in the moonlight, casting an invisible barrier that shimmered at the edge of sight, marking a seal between the living and the cursed, a symbol of protection and warding.

Lira positioned herself a few paces back, her bow drawn, an arrow tipped with silver ready in her hand. Her gaze remained fixed on the edge of the clearing, unblinking, every muscle in her body coiled like a spring, prepared for whatever might come. Voss joined her, his sword gleaming in the moonlight, a steady reminder of the task ahead.

The night seemed endless, stretching on, until at last, a sound broke the stillness – a low, guttural growl, vibrating through the air, filling the clearing with a chilling sense of dread.

From the gloom, a shape emerged, moving with an elegance that was almost sickening. It was the creature, its body twisting and writhing as though it was made of living shadow, its eyes gleaming with an unnatural light, a cunning smirk stretched across its face. It moved slowly, deliberately, as though savouring and feeding off the group's fear.

Voss felt his grip tighten on his sword, the cold steel reassuring in his hand. He forced himself to meet the creature's gaze, the darkness of its eyes pulling at him, drawing him in, probing into the very core of his soul. He could feel it searching, peeling back the layers of his mind, scanning for any vulnerability that lay buried deep within.

"Stay within the circle," Orin commanded. "Don't let anything draw you out."

The creature's gaze flicked to Orin, and its smile widened, a twisted, malicious grin that

Chapter Six

bared rows of jagged teeth. It took a step forward, testing the boundary of the circle, its form pulsing as it brushed against the edge, the air around it crackling with dark energy.

Lira raised her bow, her voice laced with tension:

"One more step, and I'll put an arrow through your heart."

The creature paused, its head tilting as though considering the threat. It laughed, a low, mocking sound that rang through the clearing, filled with a malice that caused Voss to shudder.

"You think to bind me?" it whispered, its voice hollow and rippling through Voss' mind. *"This curse is older than your blood, older than the village. It lives in the heart of the moon itself."*

"We know what you are," Voss said forcefully, willing himself not to be intimidated despite the chill that gripped him. "A guardian bound to a curse of your own making. But we can end it, release you from the moon's hold."

The creature's smile faded as it regarded Voss with a bleak, calculating gaze.

"Release me? You cannot even comprehend the price of freedom," it chided, its voice ever unpleasant, twisting through Voss' thoughts.

The creature's form shifted, dark tendrils extending from its body, wrapping around the edges of the circle, testing the strength of the binding.

"Get back," Orin said firmly, raising his hand.

The creature laughed again, louder this time, its voice tinged with threatening amusement.

"You cannot hold me forever. The moon's curse is stronger than anything you could ever imagine – even in your wildest nightmares."

The words struck something deep within Voss. A wave of dread washed over him, a promise of suffering. He had to consciously push the feeling aside, focusing on the task at hand.

"We'll end it, one way or another."

For a moment, the creature was silent, its gaze locked onto Voss', as though searching for something. Then, with a snarl, it lunged forward, slamming into the edge of the circle, the force of its rage rippling through the ground, shaking the very air. Voss felt the impact reverberate through his bones, but he held his ground, his sword raised, ready to fight.

The creature recoiled, hissing, its form shuddering as the binding forced it back. Orin's chanting, which had started as murmurs, grew louder, his voice steady and strong. The words formed a barrier of light and strength, holding the creature beyond the circle's confines.

But Voss could see the strain in Orin's face, the sweat that beaded on his brow, the tremor in his hands. The binding was strong, but the creature was stronger, a force that seemed to draw power from the moonlight itself, feeding on it, growing more solid with each passing moment.

Lira's arrow was trained on the creature's heart, her eyes narrowed with deadly focus.

"Hold still," she whispered, barely audible.

The creature twisted, its form flickering between solidity and shadow as it strained against the circle, its eyes blazing crimson with fury. For a moment, it seemed to dissolve, its shape rippling as though ready to pass through the binding, but the circle held, shimmering with Orin's magic, repelling the dark energy. Voss could feel the tension, the abundance of the creature's rage pressing down on them, the curse pulsing in the ground beneath their feet.

The creature turned to face Lira, its mouth bending into a cruel sneer.

"You think your silver can save you?" Voss heard it say mockingly, the words dripping with contempt. *"You are nothing but mere shadows to me, bound to your mortal fate. But here, under the sacred moon, I am eternal."*

"Then let's see what eternity looks like when it's shattered," Voss said, fuelled by sheer determination.

With a furious battle cry, he lunged forward, his sword gleaming as he swung it towards the creature. At the same time, Lira released her arrow, the silver tip flashing in the moonlight as it struck the creature's chest. A scream erupted from the creature, high and piercing, filling the night with a sound that sent even the ravens into a frenzy above, their cries merging into a chaotic symphony.

The creature's form buckled, shadows peeling away like smoke to reveal glimpses of a face twisted in agony – half human, half something far darker, far older. Its eyes met Voss', filled with a desperation that sent a chill through him. For a fleeting instant, Voss thought he saw something in those eyes: regret, perhaps, or something more – something that mirrored his own fear.

Then, with a final scream, the creature's form shattered entirely, the shadows unravelling into tendrils of smoke that weaved their way into the night, dispersing into the light of the sacred moon.

The clearing fell silent, but the oppressive weight persisted, a lasting presence that clung to the air. The faint glow of the altar's runes flickered as the trio stood tense, their breaths ragged and their bodies drained. Voss lowered his sword, his eyes fixed on the spot where the creature had been, his heart still hammering in his chest. The creature was gone – for now – but the unease remained. The curse still lingered, a constant reminder that the bond to the moon had not yet been severed.

Orin wiped a hand across his brow, his face pale.

"It's not over," he muttered, glancing at Voss and Lira. "It will return unless we break the curse."

As the group prepared to leave the clearing, the glow of the runes faded, the shadows creeping back into the forest. The curse was still pulsing, still alive.

Chapter Seven

The path back to the village felt longer in the quiet aftermath of the fight. Voss, Lira and Orin moved through the forest with purpose, each step a reminder of the burden of the curse that lingered over Crow's Perch. The silence between them was heavy, not from fear or tension, but from the shared understanding that the battle they'd faced was most likely only the beginning.

They reached the edge of the village just as the first hint of dawn touched the sky, casting faint hues of grey and lavender over the mist-cloaked rooftops. The villagers were still hidden behind their doors and windows, tormented eyes peering out to watch the hunters pass.

Inside the meeting hall, the elder awaited the group once more. Standing by the window, his back to the door, he watched as the early morning light crept across the horizon. His shoulders sagged under the weight of years of secrets and sins, his form nearly swallowed by the sable robes draped over him.

"We wounded the creature," Voss began, breaking the silence as they entered, his voice edged with frustration. "But it will return. The curse is woven into the moon's very light; it can't be severed by force alone."

The elder turned slowly, weary but engaged.

"I feared this would be the case," he said. "The curse is older than you can imagine, bound to the moon by blood – blood from the village's past, from choices made in desperation and regret… There is one way to break it, but it demands a price."

"So the villagers bound that guardian to the moon at the cost of their own humanity?" said Lira, barely containing her annoyance. "And now, it haunts you all. If the curse requires a price, the village must be willing to pay it."

The elder's face tightened, and for a moment,

he looked impossibly old, weakened with sorrow.

"It's not that simple," he said. "The village is bound to the curse, yes, but to sever it, it seems that a sacrifice is needed – a soul, willingly given, to take the place of the one bound to the moon."

"So that's it?" said Orin, his voice tinged with bitter disbelief. "One of us trades places with that creature? Becomes the next soul bound to the sacred moon?"

"Indeed, it would now seem that way," the elder said solemnly. "I was hoping that it wouldn't have to come to this... The moon demands a guardian, and if none is given willingly, the curse will continue, claiming more lives, growing stronger. Perhaps there is one of you willing to be braver than us all."

Voss could feel his pulse quickening, the reality of their mission settling over him with finality. He had joined this fight expecting to hunt a beast, to end a tangible threat that plagued innocent lives. But now, he saw that the curse was not a simple spell to be broken; it was a pact, an agreement with darkness that demanded balance, a cycle of sacrifice and suffering.

"Are you saying we should just offer ourselves up?" Orin said angrily, addressing the elder with shock and defiance. "We didn't come here to become sacrifices!"

"This is awful," said Lira. "If we don't break the curse, it will consume this village and everyone in it."

Voss knew Lira was right; they couldn't leave the curse unbroken. But the thought of offering himself, of surrendering his life to the darkness, was a sacrifice he wasn't sure he was prepared to make. He had spent years fighting the shadows, hunting creatures that fed on fear and despair. But this? This was different. This was a choice, one that demanded everything he had to give.

"Tell us what we need to do," he said, meeting the elder's gaze after a long pause.

"Tonight, under the full moon, you must return to the clearing where the creature was bound. You must draw it forth, weaken it, and then, one of you must step into the circle and willingly give your soul to take its place. It is a fate no one should have to face, but if the curse is to end, the moon must have its guardian."

Orin muttered something under his breath, his jaw clenched as he turned away. Voss could see the conflict in his expression, the horror and anger warring within him, but he knew that Orin's heart, like his own, was bound by a sense of duty stronger than any fear. They had come to Crow's Perch to end the darkness, and if this was the only way, they would face it together.

As they left the meeting hall, Lira fell into step beside Voss.

"I know this isn't what any of us expected," she murmured, "but we can't leave the curse to fester. Not after what we've seen."

"Indeed," said Voss, his mind racing. "We'll return to the clearing tonight. I'll do whatever it takes to keep the curse from spreading, but… if it comes down to it, I won't ask either of you to sacrifice yourselves. This is my burden to bear."

"We're in this together, Voss," Lira insisted. "Don't forget that."

Orin trailed a few steps behind them, his thoughts hidden beneath a mask of quiet resolve. Voss could sense his reluctance, the anger that simmered beneath his exterior, but he also knew that Orin's loyalty ran deep. Whatever lay ahead, they would face it together, bound by a shared purpose and the knowledge that their choices would live on through Crow's Perch long after they were gone.

***

The sun was setting by the time they made their final preparations, each of them lost in their own thoughts. The village was still, the streets empty, as though the very air was waiting for night to fall. With a difficult sense of finality hanging over him, Voss checked his sword, his fingers brushing over the worn leather grip, a reminder of every battle he had fought, every bleak path he had walked.

As the first stars appeared in the twilight sky, the trio set off towards the forest once more. Voss could feel the sacred moon rising, its presence cold and watchful as it followed them into the woods.

The path wound deeper into the heart of the forest, the trees towering above them like ancient sentinels, their branches stretching out like arms, casting unsettling shapes across the ground. The air grew colder, filled with the scent of loamy earth and the faint tang of decay.

As they neared the clearing, Voss felt a strange calm settle over him, a sense of acceptance mingling with the sick feeling of dread that roiled in his stomach. He glanced at Lira and Orin, seeing the same resolve reflected in their faces, an understanding that bound them together in a way that no words could capture.

Tonight, under the light of the sacred moon, they would face the darkness one final time. Whatever the cost, they would see it through to the end.

Chapter Eight

Voss led the way, his steps steady but heavy, as though each one carried the burden of a thousand choices. The knowledge of what lay ahead, of the sacrifice demanded by the curse, pressed on him like a physical weight, but he forced himself to keep moving. As a hunter, a protector, this was the path he had chosen.

Behind him, Lira moved with a quiet grace. Sharp and alert, with her bow slung across her back, she walked with purpose, unflinching. Voss could sense the strength in her, the resolve that had carried her through countless battles, but tonight, there was something more – an acceptance, a readiness that mirrored his own.

Orin brought up the rear, his steps slower, more hesitant. He muttered to himself, fragments of old incantations, spells of protection that had long lost their potency in the face of the curse's ancient power. Voss knew that Orin's loyalty ran deep, that beneath the layers of scepticism and bitterness lay a heart bound by duty. But he could also sense Orin's reluctance, the fear that gripped him, a reminder of the fragile line between courage and despair.

When they reached the edge of the clearing, they were met by the familiar sight of the stone altar standing in the centre, bathed in the cold light of the sacred moon. The runes carved into its surface glowed faintly, pulsing with a rhythm that seemed almost hypnotic.

The clearing was empty, but Voss could feel the presence of the creature, lurking just beyond sight, watching from obscurity. It was there, waiting, as though aware of the ritual about to unfold.

"This is it," Voss said to his companions as he took a step closer to the altar. "Whatever happens tonight, we face it together. No one turns back."

"We came to break the curse, and that's

exactly what we'll do," Lira said fiercely. "We know the cost."

Orin looked between them, a flicker of alarm in his eyes, but he nodded, his jaw set in determination.

"If this is how it ends," he said, "then let's make it count."

Voss moved to the edge of the altar, placing his sword on the ground beside it, a gesture of surrender and readiness. He reached out, tracing his fingers over the runes, feeling the thrum of ancient magic beneath his touch. The air around him grew colder, thicker, as though the forest was closing in, watching, waiting for the moment when blood would be spilled, and the curse would take its toll.

Voss glanced at Orin, who was already pulling a small vial from his satchel – a mixture of herbs and silver dust, the last of his supplies. Orin poured it in a circle around the altar, the powder shimmering in the moonlight, forming a boundary that would either trap the creature or buy them enough time to complete the ritual.

He began to chant, low and steady, a rhythm that thrummed through the clearing, filling the air with a sense of anticipation. Lira moved to her position, her bow drawn, an arrow tipped with silver ready in her hand.

Voss picked up his sword, listening attentively to Orin's chant, each word a plea to the sacred moon, a call to the ancient powers that held the forest in their grasp. He could feel the energy building, a crackling force filling the air, growing stronger with each passing moment, drawing the creature towards them like a moth to a flame.

And then, the shadows shifted.

A low growl reverberated through the clearing, vibrating through the ground, filling the air with a sense of dread that clung to the group like a shroud. Voss' hand tightened around the hilt of his sword, and he held his ground, forcing himself to stand firm as the creature emerged from the darkness.

It was larger now, its form more solid, more defined, as though the moonlight had given it strength. Its eyes burned with a raging fire,

Chapter Eight

red and unblinking, filled with a malice that couldn't be unseen. The creature moved slowly, smoothly, its twisted form shifting and writhing, tendrils of shadow curling around it like smoke.

Lira drew her bowstring back, the silver-tipped arrow glinting in the moonlight.

"We end this tonight," she whispered, her voice barely more than a breath.

The creature's gaze flicked to her, an unpleasant smile spreading across its face, filled with a mocking amusement.

"You dare to challenge the curse?" Voss heard it say, its voice a raspy hiss. *"This power is older than you, older than the village. It lives in the heart of the moon, and you are nothing but a fleeting wind before it."*

Voss felt a surge of defiance rising within him, a fierce determination.

"We're here to break the cycle," he said firmly. "Whatever you were, whatever power bound you to the moon, it ends tonight."

The creature's expression hardened, its form shifting, contorting as it drew closer, testing the boundary of the silver circle. The powder flared, creating a barrier that held it back, but Voss could see the strain in Orin's face, the tremor in his hands as he struggled to keep the creature away.

Lira loosed her arrow, the silver tip slicing through the air and striking the creature in the shoulder. A scream erupted from its twisted form, a sound filled with rage and agony, as though the arrow had pierced something far deeper than flesh. The creature recoiled, shadows peeling away from its body, revealing a glimpse of the human it had once been – a face distorted by pain and sorrow, eyes hollow and haunted.

For a brief moment, Voss thought he saw something familiar in those eyes – a spark of recognition, a flicker of the soul that inhabited the twisted form before him. But the moment passed, and the creature's rage returned, its form solidifying once more as it lunged towards them, slamming into the boundary with a force that sent tremors through the ground.

Chapter Eight

Orin staggered back, his chant faltering. The circle flickered, the silver powder dimming as the creature's ominous form pressed against the boundary, relentless and unyielding.

"Hold the line!" Voss shouted, his voice cutting through the chaos.

He raised his sword, stepping forward to face the creature, his attention locked onto its haunting face and the traces of humanity that lingered within.

"You cannot break the curse," the creature insisted, its voice a loud, unpleasant whisper that slithered through Voss' mind. *"You shall be bound to it, as am I."*

Voss forced himself not to waver, to push past the horror that threatened to overwhelm him. He tightened his grip on his sword, its familiar reliability a comfort amidst the chaos.

"We'll sever this bond, no matter the cost," he vowed under his breath. "Your time is over."

Lira fired another arrow, striking the creature near its chest, though not in a spot that seemed to cause it any significant pain. Nevertheless, it staggered, its form shuddering as it struggled to maintain its shape.

The runes on the altar glowed brighter, a signal that the ritual was reaching its peak. Orin's voice rose, his chant growing louder, more powerful, the words a barrier against the creature's rage. The boundary shimmered with a light that grew stronger, more intense, as though the forest itself was lending its strength to the ritual.

The creature's gaze locked onto Orin, its eyes gleaming with a sinister intelligence. With a snarl, it lunged, striking with a force that sent Orin staggering, his knees buckling as he fought to stay upright. Voss moved without hesitation, stepping in front of him, his sword raised, his stance unyielding.

"Stay behind the circle, Orin," he commanded urgently. "The creature is trying to break your concentration. Don't let it."

Orin nodded, his face pale but determined. He steadied himself, his voice rising once more in a chant that grew stronger, more

Chapter Eight

forceful, the words laced with defiance.

"You cannot kill me," the creature said, its voice hissing and carrying centuries of suffering and rage through Voss' mind. *"This curse is older than any of you, older than the village. I am bound to the moon, to the blood that has stained this ground. And you... you are nothing but sacrifices."*

"We're here to end this," Voss said, forcing himself to reject the images of bleakness and death that clawed at his mind. "Your hold over this place, over these people: it ends tonight."

The creature seemed to draw power from the very moonlight itself – feeding from it, taking strength from it. The shadows around it grew more defined, taking on shapes that seemed almost human, faces frozen in silent screams, hands reaching out, raking at the edge of the circle.

Orin's chant wavered, his voice trembling under the intensity of the creature's presence. Voss could see the strain in his face, the exhaustion that lined his features, but he also saw the fire in his eyes, the dedication that drove him forward, pushing him to keep going, to cling to the fraying threads of his strength.

"Stay strong, Orin," Lira called out.

The creature's form shifted again, and this time, it turned to look at Lira.

"So brave," it said, its voice a soft, mocking hiss in Voss' mind. *"But bravery won't save you from the fate that awaits you. The moon's curse demands blood, and it will have yours."*

"If blood is what it wants, then it will have to fight for it," Lira replied, unflinching.

She raised her bow, drawing back an arrow, her hand steady, her aim true. When she released, the arrow struck the creature in the chest, embedding itself deep within the writhing shadows. The creature screamed, its form shuddering, flickering between solid and smoke, its face twisting in agony. Voss could sense the creature's power weakening, unravelling under the force of their combined strength.

Orin's chant grew louder, stronger, the words

filling the air with a sense of finality, a power that seemed to cut through the darkness, reaching into the heart of the curse. The creature writhed, its form collapsing, shrinking, as though the very shadows that composed it were being drawn back, reclaimed by the forest, by the earth.

Certain that the creature was significantly weakened – its movements slower, its form flickering as if struggling to hold itself together – Voss felt a surge of confidence that the tide had turned. Gripping his sword tightly, he let out a battle cry and charged forward, closing the distance immediately.

As Voss' blade plunged into the creature's chest, a blinding light erupted from the wound, searing through the night. Voss instinctively recoiled, shielding his eyes from the intense radiance that flooded the area, overwhelming him with its painful brightness. The deafening wail of the creature pierced the air, and just as Voss managed to squint against the diminishing light, he witnessed its menacing form shattering into ghostly shards, dissipating into nothingness.

Slowly but surely, the air grew still. Still in shock, Voss staggered back. He looked to Lira and Orin, noticing the exhaustion on their faces, but also the spark of relief and triumph beginning to ignite within them.

"It's over," said Orin, his voice filled with a mixture of disbelief and awe. "The creature is gone. We did it."

But Voss felt no relief, only a strange, unpleasant emptiness, as though a piece of himself had been left behind, taken by the creature.

Lira moved to his side.

"Are you alright?" she asked worriedly.

Voss nodded, forcing a smile, though he could feel something horrible lingering at the edges of his thoughts.

"It's over," he said, though his voice held a hint of doubt.

They turned, wearily leaving the clearing behind, but as the moonlight followed them, something felt wrong, unfinished.

Chapter Nine

A week had crawled by since Voss, Orin and Lira had emerged from the forest, battered but victorious – or so they had thought. The air that night had been sharp with a fragile triumph, and yet, even as they had stepped beyond the oppressive hold of the treeline, an unease had gnawed at Voss' thoughts. Something about their victory felt too clean, too convenient.

The elder's macabre warnings had played on his mind: the curse demanded a sacrifice. Yet, as they had stood in the pale moonlight, intact and breathing, the dire predictions had almost seemed like empty theatrics. For a fleeting moment, Voss had dared to hope the elder's words were exaggerated – perhaps born of fear or ignorance. But that hope had been thin, fragile as frost on a winter morning. Deep in his gut, an instinct had whispered: this wasn't over.

Several days later, sitting in the cramped, dimly lit room he'd rented at the Crow's Perch tavern, Voss understood why the forest hadn't let him go so easily. The illness had taken root, insidious and unrelenting. At first, he had dismissed it as mere exhaustion – after all, the battle had been gruelling, and sleep had been elusive. But this was no ordinary fatigue. His body betrayed him, his muscles like lead, a burning fever searing his skin even as waves of shivering wracked him. Hunger fled, nausea lingered, and sleep brought no reprieve, only nightmares where the creature's face leered at him through the haze in his mind.

The hallucinations were close to unbearable: ghostly outlines flickering in the corners of his vision, the sound of a guttural laugh haunting his ears. He had seen the creature's eyes in his dreams – glaring, unblinking, filled with malice – its presence like a phantom hand on his chest.

At first, Voss had tried to hide his symptoms, brushing off Orin's pointed comments and Lira's soft enquiries. But the illness grew stronger, hollowing him out, fraying the edges of his resolve. Now, there was no hiding it.

Chapter Nine

Unable to deny the reality of the situation any longer, Voss summoned Orin and Lira to his room. As his companions sat across from him, their concern thickening the air, the dim candlelight threw shaded patterns over their faces, and for a moment, the room felt oppressively small. Sitting across from them on his bed, Voss leaned forward, clasping his hands tightly, his knuckles white against his reddened skin.

"Something's wrong," he said, getting straight to the point, his voice raspy and weak. "This isn't exhaustion. It's something else."

His gaze met Lira's first. Her eyes were wide, searching, the worry she didn't voice etched clearly on her face. Then he looked to Orin, whose expression was sharp and focused, his jaw clenched with barely restrained frustration.

"Why didn't you tell us sooner?" Lira asked as she leaned forward in her chair, her tone measured but tinged with an edge of hurt. "We could have done something."

"I thought it would pass," Voss said, not quite convinced of his own words. "I didn't want to cause any alarm, but it's not getting better. The fever, the hallucinations... it's like the creature is still with me. When I drove my sword through it, I felt... something – like it was leaving a piece of itself behind."

Orin stood abruptly, his chair scraping against the wooden floor. He began to pace, his movements restless, his anger barely contained.

"I knew there was something off about this," he said, his voice taut with fury. "Something just doesn't add up."

"What are you suggesting?" Lira asked, nervously wringing her hands in her lap.

"The elder..." Orin replied bitterly. "I'm sorry, but there's just something about him that I don't trust. It feels as though he sent us on a fruitless errand, and that the curse is as present as ever."

Voss exhaled slowly, his mind struggling through the fog of fever.

"So what now?" he asked, too fatigued to come up with a plan unaided.

Chapter Nine

"I know someone," Orin said, abruptly halting his pacing. "There's a witch – Zelfara. She lives in Naria, a few villages over. If anyone can tell us what's happening to you, it's her."

"And you trust her?" Lira asked, tilting her head.

"With my life," Orin said firmly. "She's old, powerful, and holds no emotional ties to Crow's Perch. She has no stake in the village. She will tell us what we need to know, and at the very least, if Voss is carrying the curse, she'll know how to help him through it, if only a little."

Voss closed his eyes for a moment, assessing the risks against the gnawing terror of the unpleasant sensations clawing at the crevices of his mind.

"Then we go to Naria," he said finally. "If this witch can help, I'll take that chance."

***

The journey to Naria was brutal. The bitter air taunted their skin, and the road was long, every step wearing at their frayed nerves. Voss moved like a man carrying a mountain on his back, each day draining more of his strength. By the time they reached the village, the exhaustion in his bones felt permanent.

Zelfara's home stood at the edge of a quiet clearing, a modest structure cloaked in wild ivy and flanked by ancient trees. Its worn stone walls radiated a strange tranquillity, and the air around it smelt of earth and herbs. Smoke drifted lazily from the chimney, a subtle promise of warmth.

As they approached, Voss was struck by a sudden sense of awe, his steps faltering slightly and not just from his exhaustion. This was no ordinary witch's house; it felt alive, pulsing with magic, as though the energy within the walls was drawing him in, calling out to something he hadn't expected to feel.

Orin pushed ahead without hesitation, striding up to the front door with purpose. He rapped loudly on its painted-but-chipped wooden surface, causing Voss to jump in surprise.

Chapter Nine

After a few moments of waiting, the door slowly creaked open to reveal a wizened woman standing before them. Her hair was pure white, and her eyes seemed to pierce through them with an intensity that might have unsettled others. But as Voss met her gaze, a strange sense of ease washed over him, as though he'd found something familiar in her presence.

"Orin?" she said, clearly not used to having visitors, but at ease all the same. "What brings you to my humble abode?"

"We seek your help, Zelfara," said Orin, stepping forward and bowing respectfully.

Zelfara's eyes flickered over Orin and Lira before settling on Voss. Upon studying him more closely, her expression softened into one of sympathy.

"Come inside," she said simply, turning and walking serenely into her home.

Voss followed behind Orin and Lira as they entered through the doorway. The inside of Zelfara's home was dimly lit by candles that flickered throughout various rooms. Shelves lined every wall, filled with potions, herbs, and books – countless volumes dedicated to various magical practices.

"Please, take a seat," Zelfara said, gesturing to a large armchair in front of the fireplace.

Voss hesitated for a moment before sinking into its soft cushions, letting the warmth of the fire wash over him. Orin and Lira took seats on either side of him, their faces etched with concern.

Zelfara settled into a chair across from them, her posture straight and regal. She studied Voss intently for a moment before speaking.

"What troubles you, young one?" she asked kindly.

Voss recounted the events in halting detail. His voice was hoarse, the words faltering as the memories haunted him: the creature's twisted form, the elder's cryptic warnings, the sickness that had followed. As he spoke, Zelfara listened intently, her expression growing more concerned with each word.

"You haven't broken the curse," she said

finally, her tone sombre. "You've severed a piece of it, but the rest remains – and now, it has latched onto you. Also, I'm sorry to say this, but if I had to stake my life on it, I'd say the elder sent you into that forest knowing full well you'd return with the curse still intact."

Her words struck like a blow, leaving the room silent except for the crackle of the fire. Voss felt Lira's hand on his arm, steadying him. Orin, meanwhile, had risen to his feet, his anger a tangible force.

"I knew it!" he said. "That elder set us up."

"Curses like this often serve those in power," Zelfara said, her words tinged with regret. "Fear keeps people loyal, pliable. By sending hunters into the forest on false promises every so often, the elder maintains a façade for the villagers. It's likely he is behind the curse entirely. While he may not have started it, it's plausible that maintaining it serves his interests. I've seen things like this before."

The revelation landed less like a sudden thunderclap and more like the grim echo of a truth they had all quietly feared. The impact of the witch's words settled heavily in the room.

The elder of Crow's Perch, it seemed, was no hapless bystander in the village's plight. He was the architect of its suffering, a manipulator wielding fear with the precision of a craftsman. As Zelfara had explained, the panic of others lent itself to intoxicating power, capable of binding people under the rule of those who claimed to offer protection. To sustain that control, the curse had to endure. Voss felt a cold fury rising within him, tempered only by the gnawing sickness that sapped his strength.

"Please," Zelfara said tenderly, her voice cutting through the increasing tension. "Take a moment to think. I'll fetch some tea. Perhaps clarity will come with it."

Without waiting for a response, the witch excused herself with a grace that spoke of her years of experience dealing with troubled souls. She slipped into the kitchen, her departure leaving the group to confront their collective unease in her absence.

The hearth fire crackled softly, throwing

Chapter Nine

flickering patterns onto the weathered walls. Orin, ever the one to shatter silences, sat back down and leaned forward to address the others.

"Zelfara's right," he said, his hands clasped tightly together as though holding back the tide of his anger. "We can trust her. She's never steered me wrong."

"We don't have much of a choice," said Lira, her words steady but tinged with melancholy. "If Zelfara can help, then we need to listen to her."

Voss lifted his head slowly, the firelight catching the sheen of sweat on his brow.

"Something felt wrong about this from the start," he admitted, his voice strained but resolute. "The elder's reluctance to be clear with us, the way the creature seemed impossible to defeat."

"We did our best with what we knew at the time," said Lira, placing a hand on Voss' shoulder.

The room lapsed into silence once more, the

three of them bound together in their shared sense of betrayal. Outside, the wind howled through the trees, its mournful wail amplifying the crushing anguish of their thoughts.

When Zelfara returned, balancing a tray of steaming tea, her expression remained composed, but the sharpness in her eyes revealed her deep awareness of the trio's turmoil. She set the tray down on the low table, gesturing for them to take a cup.

"Please, stay here for a few nights," she said, her voice caring yet firm. "You'll need your strength. It takes time to lift a curse from a soul, and I insist on keeping an eye on you for a while after. Besides, it's best you stay away from Crow's Perch for now – at least until you have a clear plan of how to proceed."

Chapter Ten

The air in Zelfara's small house was laden with the quiet of the early morning, the only sound the creak of the old floorboards and the faint rustle of leaves against the window. Upstairs, in the cramped spare room, Voss lay on the bed, his chest rising and falling in shallow breaths. His face was pale, slick with sweat, his body trembling faintly under the covers.

On the floor, Lira and Orin had made makeshift camp beds, their rest fitful as they kept an ear attuned to the sound of Voss' laboured breathing. Lira stirred, her sharp senses jolting her awake as the first pale light of dawn seeped in through the curtains. She sat up slowly, rubbing the sleep from her eyes before immediately turning her attention to Voss. He hadn't stirred all night, and his pallor was worse.

Orin, his head propped on a rolled cloak, muttered something incoherent in his sleep before turning over with a faint groan. Lira glanced at him, then back at Voss, her lips pressed into a thin line. The room smelt faintly of herbs and sweat, a reminder of the night's restless vigil.

A knock at the door broke the quiet. It was soft but firm, a deliberate sound that immediately brought both Orin and Lira to full alertness.

"It's time," came Zelfara's voice, calm and steady.

Orin was already pushing himself to his feet, his movements stiff from the hard floor. Lira followed, casting one last glance at Voss before stepping to the door and pulling it open. Zelfara stood in the dim hallway, her white hair like a halo in the faint morning light. Her expression was serene but serious, her presence commanding.

"Bring him downstairs," Zelfara said, her gaze flicking past Lira to where Voss lay. "We need to act now."

Orin and Lira exchanged a brief glance before moving to the bed. Orin bent down, his hands firm but gentle as he helped Voss sit up. Voss groaned softly, his head lolling forward as though the weight of it was too much to bear.

"Easy now," Orin said, his voice low and reassuring.

"We've got you," Lira murmured, slipping her arm under Voss' to steady him.

Between them, they eased him off the bed, his legs trembling beneath him as they guided him towards the door. Each step felt like a trial, his body weak and slow to respond, his breath coming in shallow gasps.

Zelfara waited at the bottom of the stairs, watching the trio descend. The room below was bathed in a golden light from the fire burning in the hearth, the warmth contrasting with the chill that clung to the air.

When they reached the main room, Zelfara gestured towards the chair near the fire.

"Sit him there," she instructed.

They lowered Voss into the chair, his head falling back against the cushion as his eyes fluttered shut. Zelfara approached, her hand moving with practiced precision as she placed her palm against his forehead. A faint frown crossed her face, and she drew back, nodding to herself.

"We're going to the forest," she said, turning to face the others. "The curse is taking root deep within him. To extract it, I need to channel the ritual's power through a place of raw, natural energy. The forest nearby is ancient and strong – it will amplify my magic and give Voss the best chance of survival."

Confident that the group would follow her lead without question, Zelfara approached a shelf and pulled down a large deer skull with gnarled antlers. Its bleach-white surface glinted in the firelight.

"This will be the focus," she said, cradling it in her hands. "It's powerful, and exactly what we need."

***

The journey to the forest was gruelling. The trees loomed high above them, their bare branches twisting like skeletal fingers against the pale sky. The air was cold and damp, filled with the scent of moss and something faintly sweet. Voss stumbled frequently, his weight leaning heavily on Orin and Lira as they guided him along the uneven path.

Zelfara led the way, her steps confident and sure despite the rugged terrain. She carried the deer skull in one hand, her other gripping a staff carved from dark wood, its surface smooth from years of use.

The forest thickened as they went, the trees closer together, the shadows deepening. The only sounds were the crunch of leaves beneath their boots and the subtle whistle of wind through the branches.

At last, they reached a clearing. The space was wide and circular, its ground blanketed in soft viridian moss, dappled with the filtered light. Zelfara stopped in the centre, turning to face the others.

"Lay him down here," she instructed, pointing to the moss near her feet.

Orin and Lira obeyed, easing Voss onto the ground. His breathing was shallow, his skin pale and clammy. Zelfara knelt beside him, placing the deer skull at his head and the staff at his feet.

"Stand back," she told Orin and Lira. "This will not be easy."

Orin and Lira retreated to the edge of the clearing, their attention fixed on Zelfara as she prepared to begin the ritual.

The air seemed to shift as Zelfara raised her hands, her voice rising in a chant that dominated the space. The deer skull began to shine with a light that pulsed in time with her words. The wind picked up, swirling around them in a vortex that sent leaves spiralling into the air.

Voss stirred, his eyes fluttering open as a sharp gasp escaped his lips. He clutched at his chest, his body arching as if an unseen force was pulling at him.

Zelfara's voice grew louder, her chant a commanding force that seemed to shake the very ground beneath them. The deer skull glowed brighter, its antlers crackling with energy as streams of light shot out, connecting with the staff at Voss' feet.

Chapter Ten

A dark mist began to rise from Voss' body, coiling and twisting like smoke. He cried out, his voice raw with pain as the mist was drawn towards the deer skull. Zelfara's hands moved in precise gestures, guiding the energy, her eyes blazing with an intensity that left Orin and Lira awestruck.

The mist swirled around the skull until the entire clearing was bathed in an eerie light. The energy surged, and with a final, thunderous chant, Zelfara raised her arms to the heavens.

The brightest light of all burst outwards from the deer skull, blinding in its brilliance. Voss cried out one last time, arching his back and shuddering before his body went limp, collapsing into stillness.

The clearing fell silent, the wind dying down, the light fading. Zelfara knelt beside Voss, her breath coming in short gasps. She placed a hand on his chest, her expression softening.

"It's done," she said quietly.

Chapter Eleven

Zelfara's home was quiet, bathed in the warm hue of afternoon sunlight filtering in through the lace curtains. Days had passed since the ritual in the forest, and the change in Voss was undeniable. The fever that had wracked his body was gone and had been replaced with a steady strength. The colour had returned to his cheeks, and his eyes were no longer haunted by the flickering shadows of the curse.

He stood near the window, his broad shoulders framed by the light. His hand rested on the hilt of his sword, fingers absently drumming against the pommel as he stared out at the pleasant sky. His recovery had been swift, a testament to Zelfara's skill, but the newfound clarity brought with it a purpose laden with responsibility.

Behind him, Lira sat at the table, meticulously inspecting her arrows. One by one, she tested their shafts for imperfections, her movements slow and deliberate. Her expression was unreadable, her focus intense. Orin leaned against the far wall, arms crossed, foot tapping impatiently against the wooden floor. The air between them was thick with unspoken tension, the kind that came before a storm.

"We can't wait any longer," Voss said finally, his voice cutting through the silence as he turned to face them, his jaw set. "The curse may be gone from me, but it's still strangling Crow's Perch. If we don't act, the villagers will continue to suffer."

"Indeed," Orin agreed. "The elder's had his hands on this curse for too long. We know he's behind it – his lies, his manipulations. He sent us into that forest to die."

Lira set down the arrow in her hand, her gaze flicking between the two men.

"I agree," she said softly, "but if we're going back to Crow's Perch to kill the elder, I wish we could be certain. There can't be room for doubt. I know everything points to him, but you know how curses are; you know the suspicions and paranoia that can surround them. If he's not the one behind this..."

Her words trailed off, the implication hanging heavy in the room.

"You're right," Voss admitted reluctantly, pinching the bridge of his nose. "We can't afford to be wrong. But every sign points to him. The way he withheld important information, the way he pushed us into danger. It's all there."

"Certainty is not out of reach," Zelfara said, stepping into the room from her study.

"What are you suggesting?" Orin asked, turning to her with a raised eyebrow.

Zelfara gestured to a large crystal ball resting on a pedestal in the corner of the room. Its surface shimmered faintly, a subtle, unearthly light dancing within it.

"This," she said, her tone matter-of-fact. "The crystal ball is an old tool of mine, one I rarely use. But in cases such as this, where truth is vital, it can show us what we need to see."

Lira frowned slightly, the tension in her posture betraying her inner conflict.

"You're certain it will work? That it'll show us the truth?"

"The ball does not lie," Zelfara said, calm and confident. "It reveals what is, free from bias or manipulation. If the elder is guilty, you will see it. If he is not, you will see that."

They all gathered around the crystal ball, the air humming with an electric tension. Zelfara moved with deliberate precision, lighting candles at each corner of the pedestal and scattering a circle of finely ground herbs around the base. The scent was sharp and invigorating, a mixture of sage and something more arcane.

"Focus on your questions," Zelfara instructed as she placed her hands on the crystal ball. "The magic will do the rest."

The room fell silent. The light in the crystal ball grew brighter, its surface shifting and swirling like liquid silver.

The first image appeared, faint at first, but then sharpening into clarity. The elder's face loomed within the ball, his expression composed as he stood in the centre of the village square. The image shifted, showing him in his home, poring over ancient texts, his hands moving with a practiced ease as he traced symbols onto a sheet of parchment.

The scene changed again, and this time, a chill ran through the room. The elder stood in the forest near Crow's Perch, his form flickering and twisting. Shadows coiled around him, and his features distorted, his body elongating and darkening.

Voss' breath caught in his throat.

"That's..."

"The creature," Lira finished, her voice filled with disbelief.

The crystal ball revealed the transformation in stark detail. The elder's body contorted, his face stretching into the grotesque visage of the creature that had haunted them in the forest. His eyes glowed with an unholy light, and his hands became talons, his form wreathed in shadow.

The ball continued to show more: villagers trembling as the creature stalked the forest, the elder returning to the village as if nothing had happened, his human guise a mask that hid the truth. The montage painted a damning picture, one that left no room for doubt. The elder had been their enemy all along, a wolf in sheep's clothing, and now, the truth was clear.

Zelfara lifted her hands, and the light in the crystal ball dimmed, the images fading into obscurity. She looked at the group, her expression grave.

"You have your answer."

Orin slammed a fist onto the table nearby, his anger erupting.

"Orin, calm down," Lira said, reaching out and placing a hand on his arm. "We have what we need. Now that we're certain of the elder's guilt, we can act without hesitation."

"Yes," said Voss. "He's been feeding off that curse, using it to control the village and keep them afraid. It's time to put an end to this."

"You must tread carefully," Zelfara warned, her gaze resting on Voss. "Clearly, the elder is powerful, perhaps more than you may realise. Still though, I am certain that his arrogance will be his downfall. Strike true, and do not waver."

"We leave at first light," Voss announced firmly to Orin and Lira. "Crow's Perch deserves to be free of him, and we're going to make sure it is."

Chapter Twelve

The road to Crow's Perch was shrouded in a tension that neither the crisp morning air nor the soft rustle of leaves could dispel. Voss, Orin and Lira moved with conviction, their steps deliberate as they scanned the path ahead. Each carried the weight of the mission with a solemn resolve; there could be no turning back now.

It had been days since they'd left Zelfara's house in Naria, armed with the knowledge that the elder was not just complicit in the curse, but the architect of the village's suffering. The memory of the crystal ball's revelations still burned vividly in their minds: the elder's transformation into the monstrous creature they had fought in the forest, his deliberate manipulations, his cruel, calculating intent.

Voss, walking slightly ahead, clenched his jaw as the village came into view. The sight of Crow's Perch – its crooked rooftops, the well-trodden dirt paths, the shadows stretching long in the morning light – brought a mixture of emotions: anger, determination, and a flicker of pity for the villagers who had suffered under the elder's lies.

"We do this clean," Voss said firmly. "No mistakes, no hesitation."

"Understood," Orin replied, his tone equally sharp, his hand resting on the pouch at his side, the faint clink of ritual tools concealed within.

Lira glanced between the two, her expression steady but tinged with unease.

"Let's just make sure the village sees the truth," she said. "No one deserves to live under the elder's manipulation for a moment longer."

The three moved quickly, their destination clear: the hall where the elder resided.

***

Chapter Twelve

The hall was quiet when they entered. The elder was seated at a large table near the hearth, a steaming mug in his hand. He looked up as they approached, his eyes narrowing in a blend of surprise and suspicion.

"You return," he said, his voice controlled, though a flicker of unease passed across his face. "And alive, I see. Did the curse plague you further?"

Voss didn't answer. He strode forward, his hand darting out to grab the elder by the front of his robes. The elder's mug clattered to the floor, the contents spilling in a puddle.

"What is the meaning of this?" the elder demanded, his tone rising in indignation.

"You know exactly what this is," Voss said with a growl, dragging the elder to his feet with a single, forceful motion.

"No more lies," said Orin, stepping forward, his expression hardening. "We know the truth."

The elder's eyes darted between them, his composure faltering.

"You're making a mistake," he said, sputtering. "Whatever you think you've discovered..."

"Save it," Voss snapped, hauling the elder towards the door with an iron grip fuelled by righteous fury. "You're going to face the people you've been lying to for all these years."

In the village square, the trio wasted no time. Voss shoved the elder forward, forcing him to stumble into the centre of the space. Orin stood close by, his presence a warning, while Lira moved with purpose, knocking on doors and calling out to the villagers.

"Come out!" she shouted, her voice carrying over the still morning air. "Everyone, come out! You need to see this!"

One by one, the villagers emerged, their faces etched with confusion and concern. They gathered hesitantly, murmurs rippling through the growing crowd as they saw the elder standing before them, flanked by the hunters.

"What is the meaning of this?" an older man called out, his tone sharp with offence.

Chapter Twelve

"Your elder is a liar and a murderer," Voss announced loudly, addressing the crowd. "The curse that's plagued this village for generations: it may be older than him, but he is the one who's carrying it on. He's been feeding off your fear, using the curse to keep you under his thumb."

The villagers exchanged uneasy glances, disbelief and horror mingling in their expressions.

"You dare accuse me?" the elder said, his voice dripping with resentment. "After all I've done to protect this village?"

"The elder has always kept us safe," a woman spoke up from the crowd. "How can we believe such a dreadful accusation?"

"Speak your truth," Voss demanded as he levelled the tip of his sword against the elder's neck.

The elder stood tall, but panic flickered in his eyes. He knew he was in trouble.

Before anyone could react, the elder's body began to twist and contort slightly. His limbs elongated, his skin darkened, and his face began to stretch into the grotesque visage of the creature. The crowd erupted into gasps and cries of alarm as they watched the horrifying beginnings of transformation unfolding before them.

Orin, prepared for this moment, stepped closer to the elder, his hands moving swiftly as he chanted an incantation. A circle of light flared around the elder, halting the transformation mid-shift. The creature's form flickered, caught between human and beast, its snarling expression frozen in place.

"Enough!" Orin shouted, his voice ringing with authority. "Your lies are exposed. Your power is broken."

The villagers stared in stunned silence, the truth laid bare before them. Anger replaced their fear, their voices rising in a chorus of fury.

"You betrayed us!" one man shouted.

"You let us suffer for years!" cried another.

The elder – now fully reverted to his human

Chapter Twelve

form thanks to Orin's incantation – fell to his knees, his façade of authority crumbling beneath the villagers' wrath. He looked up at Voss, desperation in his eyes.

"Please," he begged. "You don't understand..."

"I understand perfectly," said Voss, his voice cold as steel as he pressed his blade to the elder's throat.

"Do it," Lira said quietly, stepping closer to Voss. "End this. For the village."

Voss nodded, his grip on his sword tightening. His eyes locked with the elder's, an unspoken understanding passing between them. Then, in one swift motion, he shoved the blade forward, slicing effortlessly through flesh and bone as blood spilled onto the cobblestones.

The elder's eyes rolled back in his head as more blood began to dribble from the corner of his mouth – wide open and shuddering with remnants of words that would never leave his soul. In a matter of time-stopping moments, his body slumped to the ground, devoid of life. The crowd stood in shock, hushed by the unexpected turn of events.

Orin knelt beside the body, placing a hand over the still chest. After a moment, he looked up, his expression resolute.

"He's gone," he said. "And so is the curse. It's over."

Epilogue

In the days and weeks following the climactic intervention, the village began to transform. The curse was gone, its dark tendrils severed with the elder's life. For the first time in living memory, the villagers no longer cast wary glances at the rising moon. The dread that had gripped their hearts with each waxing cycle was no more, replaced by a cautious hope. Children played freely outdoors under the soft aura of twilight, their laughter ringing through streets that had once been shrouded in solitude.

The ravens – once ever-watchful with eyes that had seemed to pierce the souls of all who passed – remained perched on rooftops and gnarled branches. Their demeanour was different now though; they had ceased cawing in discordant alarm, and their restless movements had settled. They still stood sentinel, but their presence felt less like a warning, and more like a protective watch over a village reborn.

Voss, Lira and Orin were hailed as heroes, saviours who had risked their lives to bring freedom to a place long forgotten by hope. The trio accepted the warmth of the village's hospitality, but they did not linger. They had never been ones to rest for long, their calling as hunters pulling them ever onward. As much as Crow's Perch offered them safety and admiration, they knew their purpose lay on the open road, where other villages still whispered of shadows in the night. Although they knew they might never again face a curse as insidious as the one in Crow's Perch, they remained vigilant, their resolve unshaken.

As the trio left Crow's Perch, the villagers watched them go until they disappeared over the horizon. The village returned to its subtle rhythms, but the atmosphere was forever changed. The square, once silent and foreboding, bustled with life. The forest that loomed on the outskirts no longer held the same menace. And when the moon rose high, its light silver and serene, people didn't cower in its presence.

Epilogue

In the quiet moments of his travels, Voss would often glance at the moon, its light now unburdened by a curse that had once nearly consumed him. He often thought of Crow's Perch, of the people who now walked there freely. It was a reminder of what he and his companions had fought for: not glory or recognition, but the chance to bring light where darkness reigned.